Raintree is an imprint of Capstone Global Library Limited, a company incorporated in England and Wales having its registered office at 264 Banbury Road, Oxford, OX2 7DY – Registered company number: 6695582

www.raintree.co.uk
myorders@raintree.co.uk



Designed by Hilary Wacholz
Original illustrations © Capstone Global Library Limited 2022
Originated by Capstone Global Library Ltd
Printed and bound in India

978 1 3982 1355 5

**British Library Cataloguing in Publication Data**
A full catalogue record for this book is available from the British Library.

Printed and bound in India

# CONTENTS

The Library of Doom is a hidden fortress.
It holds the world's largest collection
of strange and dangerous books.

Behold the Librarian. He defends the Library – and the world – from super-villains, clever thieves and fierce monsters. Many of his adventures have remained secret. Now they can be told.

SECRET #735

BOOKS CAN FILL MINDS . . .
AND STOMACHS.

Chapter One

# LIBRARY IN THE BASEMENT

Two pupils called Ross and Star are walking down a long, **DARK** stairway.

They are following their **LIBRARIAN**, Mr Yang. The stairs lead to the basement of the school.

At the bottom of the steps is a small light next to a door.

Mr Yang smiles at the pupils. "I only let my best **READERS** in here," he says.

The door opens with a groan. Mr Yang switches on a light inside.

"Wow!" says Star. "Look at all this!"

They are standing inside a **GIANT** room. It is full of huge bookshelves.

The shelves reach up to the ceiling. In between the shelves are ladders and platforms to reach the books.

"I know you two are doing a report on VAMPIRES," Mr Yang says. "The non-fiction section is over there."

The pupils stare at the shelves as Mr Yang walks back up the staircase.

Ross steps onto a SQUEAKY ladder. "I'll start looking at the books up here," he says.

Then he sees something on the ladder's first step. It is a small, **DARK** drop.

It looks like **BLOOD**.

Chapter Two

# DARK DROPS

Ross looks more closely at the **DROP**. *Wait, that's ink,* he thinks.

Another drop of ***INK*** lies on the next ladder step. Then on the next and next.

Soon Ross reaches a platform. The **TRAIL** of drops leads to a bookshelf there.

The shelf holds a book **SPLATTERED** with ink. Ross grabs the book and opens it up.

When Ross **FLICKS** through the pages, he sees something strange.

He opens another book and sees the same thing.

"Star!" he calls. "This is weird. The glossaries are **MISSING** in these books."

Ross looks at the pages where the glossary should be.

They are blank.

Star climbs **UP** the ladder to Ross's platform.

"Look," says Ross. He gives one of the books to Star.

"There's the glossary," Star says slowly. She POINTS at the word at the top of the page. "But there aren't any terms or definitions."

Ross pulls out book after book. All the glossaries are **MISSING**.

Then Star **SCREAMS**.

Chapter Three

# WHOSE TEETH?

"Ross! Did you see this?" Star asks.

Star shows him the book's back cover.

"**TEETH MARKS!**" says Ross.

Small holes have been **PUNCHED** into the back cover.

“We should show this to Mr Yang,” says Star.

“Maybe it’s rats,” says Ross.

They hear a tiny SOUND.

CRUNCH-CRUNCH-CRUNCH-CRUNCH-CRUNCH-CRUNCH

“I don’t like rats!” says Star.

She hurries **DOWN** the ladder. Ross follows. Each of them carries a book.

They hear another sound.

It's a voice. A quiet, TREMBLING voice.

"Bring it **BAAAAAAAAACCKK**!"

"That is *not* a rat," says Star.

Chapter Four

# A GATHERING OF GHOULS

Ross and Star run towards the door. A **DARK** figure steps out of the shadows.

A tall man with pale skin **BLOCKS** their way.

He has no hair. Sharp teeth stick out from his lips. His **LONG** fingers curve like a raven's claws.

"Where are you taking those **BOOKSSSSSSS**?" the tall man hisses.

Star **THROWS** her book on the floor. "There! We were just borrowing them," she says.

The man picks up the fallen book. "This book **HASSSS** given me **SSSSO** much pleasure," he says.

He sinks his front teeth **DEEP** into the covers.

MMMMMMMMMMMMMMMMMM!

"Each new word gives me **POWER**," the tall man says.

Then they hear a familiar sound.

**RRERRRRRK!**

The man moves away as the old door **SWINGS** opens. Someone steps through.

"Mr Yang!" **SHOUT** the two friends.

The librarian smiles at them.

"I told the Ghoul you would be special," Mr Yang says.

He turns to the tall man. "These kids are such book nerds. I'm sure their **BRAINS** are full of new and delicious words!"

Chapter Five

# LIGHT CARD

"What's wrong with Mr Yang?" asks Star.

The librarian's skin looks paler. His smile is full of **SHARP** teeth.

"What will we do now?" asks Ross.

"Don't worry," says Star. "I have my LIBRARY card."

Ross stares at her. "You're kidding, right?" he says.

"It's not just **ANY** old card," says Star.

The girl **PULLS** the card from her pocket. She holds it up high.

The card shines like a spotlight.

ZZZZZZZIIIIIINNNGGG!

The Ghoul and Mr Yang close their eyes and GROWL.

They reach for the two friends with sharp **CLAWS**.

Ross and Star race back up to a platform.

"How long will that light last?" Ross asks.

"Not **LONG** enough," growls Mr Yang.

A man with a long jacket **FLOATS** down from the shadowy ceiling.

"It's already been enough," he says.

"The LIBRARIAN!" gasps Mr Yang.

"Only real librarians are allowed in here!" **SHOUTS** the hero. He opens his arms. "Now, *SEA* what I can do!"

Ross and Star hear a CRASHING sound.

CCCRRRSSSSSSSSSSSHHSSSSSSSHHHH!

A giant black wave **POURS** from the shadows.

"Here is all the INK you've ever wanted!" shouts the Librarian.

The **DARK** water slams into the Ghoul and Mr Yang.

It sweeps them away.

Then the wave pulls back into the **SHADOWS**. But the room and all its books are dry.

The Librarian has vanished.

As Ross and Star climb **OFF** the platform, they hear steps on the stairs.

"What is all that NOISE down here?" a voice asks.

The door **OPENS** and reveals Mr Yang.

"Uh, have you been upstairs all this time?" asks Star.

"Of course," says Mr Yang. "Why?"

"Are our brains full of **DELICIOUS** words?" asks Ross.

"You should come **BACK** upstairs," says Mr Yang. "I think you kids need some fresh air!"

As they leave, Ross feels **SOMETHING** in his pocket. He pulls it out.

It looks like Star's LIBRARY card. But this one has his name on it.

It **SHINES** like metal, but it isn't heavy. The card is Light.

# GLOSSARY

**definition** meaning of a word

**ghoul** evil being who enjoys doing terrible things

**glossary** part of a book that lists words used in the text and gives their meanings

**groan** low creaking sound

**platform** flat, floor-like structure that is raised into the air

**splattered** covered in wet drops

**trembling** shaking a little, often from feeling nervous, scared or excited

**vampire** from stories, a dead person that rises at night to drink the blood of living people

**vanish** pass out of sight in a quick or mysterious way

# TALK ABOUT IT

1. A creature was pretending to be Mr Yang. How did Ross and Star feel when they found out? What makes you think that?

2. Have you ever used the glossary in a book before? Was it helpful? Why or why not?

# WRITE ABOUT IT

1. Which illustration is your favourite? Why? How does it add to the story? Write two paragraphs explaining your choice.

2. There are many vampire stories. In this one, the Ghoul was a type of vampire who drank ink from books. Try writing your own vampire tale. Make sure it is exciting!

# ABOUT THE AUTHOR

Michael Dahl is an award-winning author of more than 200 books for young people. He especially likes to write scary or weird fiction. His latest series are the sci-fi adventure Escape from Planet Alcatraz and School Bus of Horrors. As a child, Michael spent lots of time in libraries. "The creepier, the better," he says. These days, besides writing, he likes travelling and hunting for the one, true door that leads to the Library of Doom.

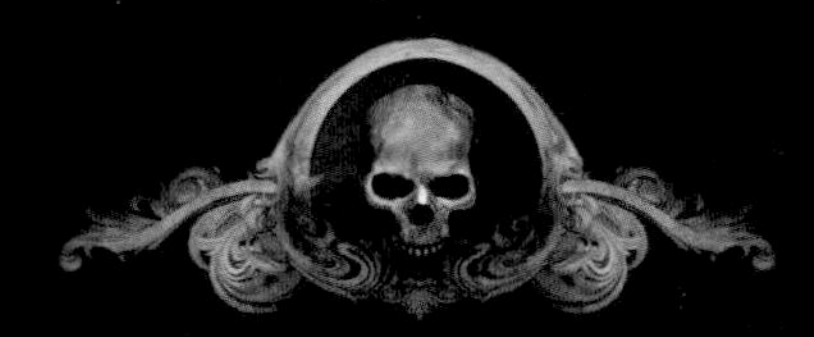

# ABOUT THE ILLUSTRATOR

Patricio Clarey was born in 1978 in Argentina. He graduated in fine arts from the Martín A. Malharro School of Visual Arts, specializing in illustration and graphic design. Patricio currently lives in Barcelona, Spain, where he works as a freelance graphic designer and illustrator. He has created several comics and graphic novels, and his work has been featured in books and other publications.